# THIS BOOK BELONGS TO

........................................................................

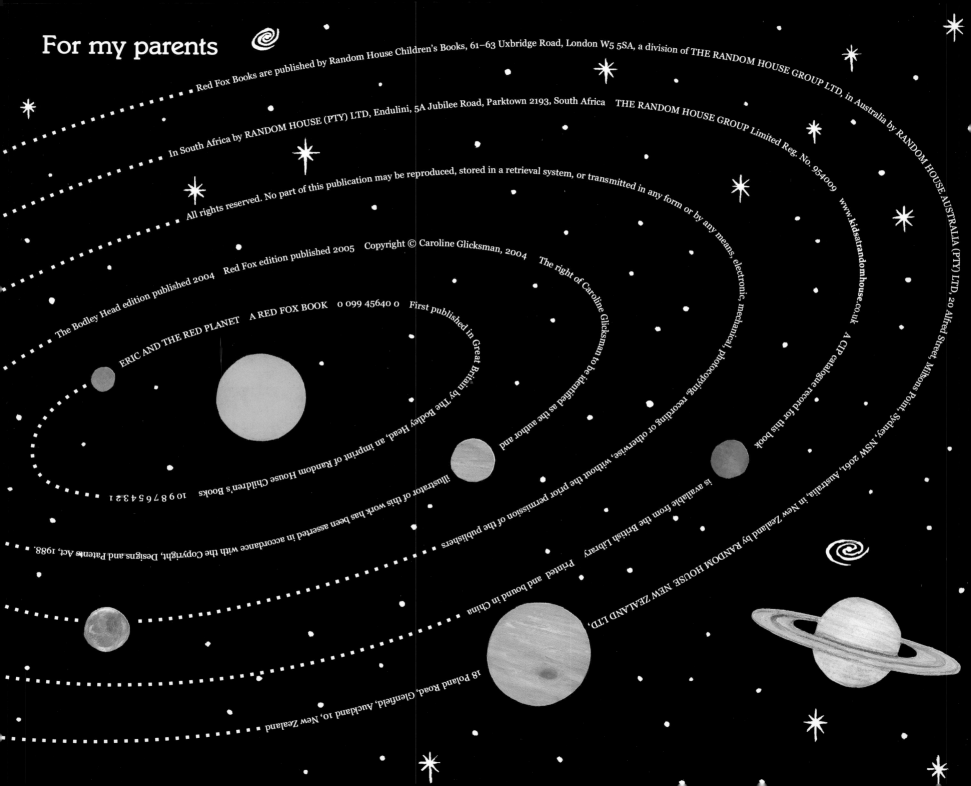

# For my parents

Red Fox Books are published by Random House Children's Books, 61–63 Uxbridge Road, London W5 5SA, a division of THE RANDOM HOUSE GROUP LTD, in Australia by RANDOM HOUSE AUSTRALIA (PTY) LTD, 20 Alfred Street, Milsons Point, Sydney, NSW 2061, Australia, in New Zealand by RANDOM HOUSE NEW ZEALAND LTD, 18 Poland Road, Glenfield, Auckland 10, New Zealand

In South Africa by RANDOM HOUSE (PTY) LTD, Endulini, 5A Jubilee Road, Parktown 2193, South Africa    THE RANDOM HOUSE GROUP Limited Reg. No. 954009    www.kidsatrandomhouse.co.uk

The Bodley Head edition published 2004    Red Fox edition published 2005    Copyright © Caroline Glicksman, 2004    The right of Caroline Glicksman to be identified as the author and illustrator of this work has been asserted in accordance with the Copyright, Designs and Patents Act, 1988.

ERIC AND THE RED PLANET    A RED FOX BOOK    0 099 45640 0    First published in Great Britain by The Bodley Head, an imprint of Random House Children's Books

A CIP catalogue record for this book is available from the British Library

Printed and bound in China

10 9 8 7 6 5 4 3 2 1

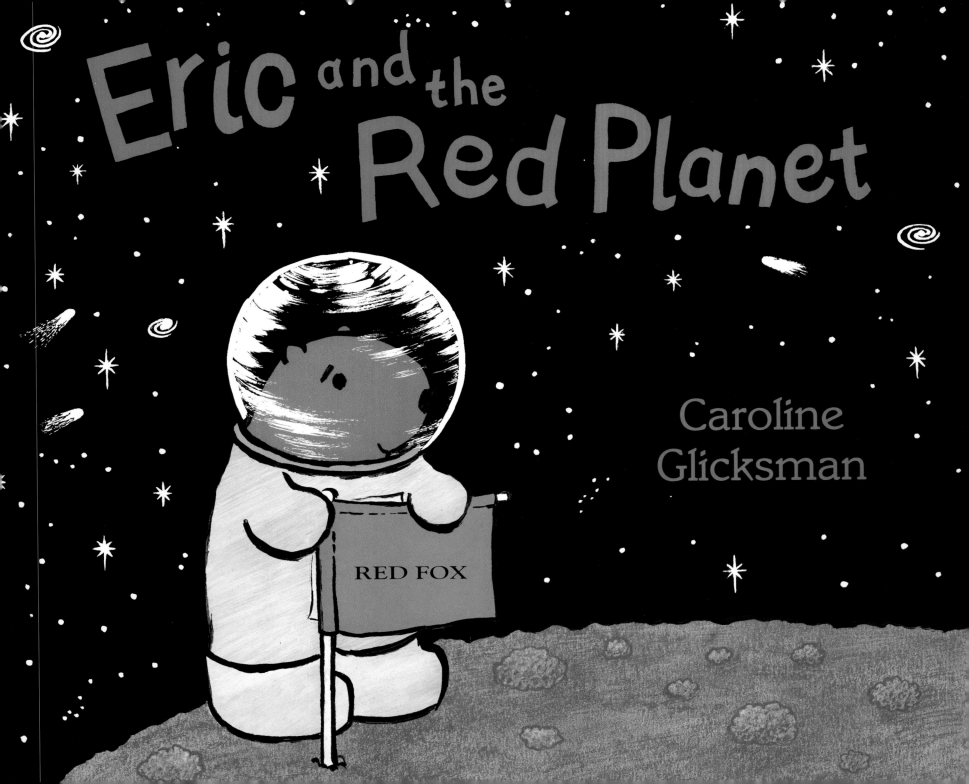

Eric is a very unusual bear.
He's red and he's very,
very clever, especially
with numbers.

He loves numbers
as much as he
loves honey.

So put honey
and numbers
together and you
get Eric's dream
breakfast – a bowl of
Honey Number Puffs.

HONEY NUMBER PUFFS™

... an
historic
day ...

THE GROWLER

MARS
LIFT-OFF
TODAY

PROBABILITY
IN PRACTICE

TRAVEL

Every morning, Eric has a special way of adding up his breakfast cereal.

8 + 2
9 + 1    7 + 3
6 + 4
5 + 5

10 + 10 + 10 + 10 + 10 +

50

But this morning,
a card
fell into
his
bowl.

Please turn over

It said:

CONGRATULATIONS!
You are eating the millionth box of **HONEY NUMBER PUFFS**™!
Bring a friend to the SpaceBear Space Base and enjoy a day in a million!

For the first time ever, Eric didn't add up his breakfast. He didn't even eat it!

Instead he rushed to the phone . . .

. . . and ten minutes later, he was scooting out of town with his best friend Erica, the only bear he has ever met who loves numbers as much as he does.

The space base was very exciting. Eric and Erica were given their very own space suits and shown around by a very important bear.
They saw:

TEN
computers
in mission
control

NINE
posters of
different
planets

EIGHT
astronauts
training

SEVEN
busy robot
bears

SIX
saws in
the rocket
workshop

FOUR
bears
carrying
clipboards

THREE
boxes of
space
biscuits

TWO
bears
pushing
scooters

FIVE
bears
painting
rockets

Mission Control

1. Mercury

2. Venus

5. Jupiter

6. Saturn

7. Uranus

Space biscuits

Space biscuits

WARNING:
EXTREMELY
TASTY

. . . and one huge tank
of honey, the very
best fuel for sending
bear rockets into space.

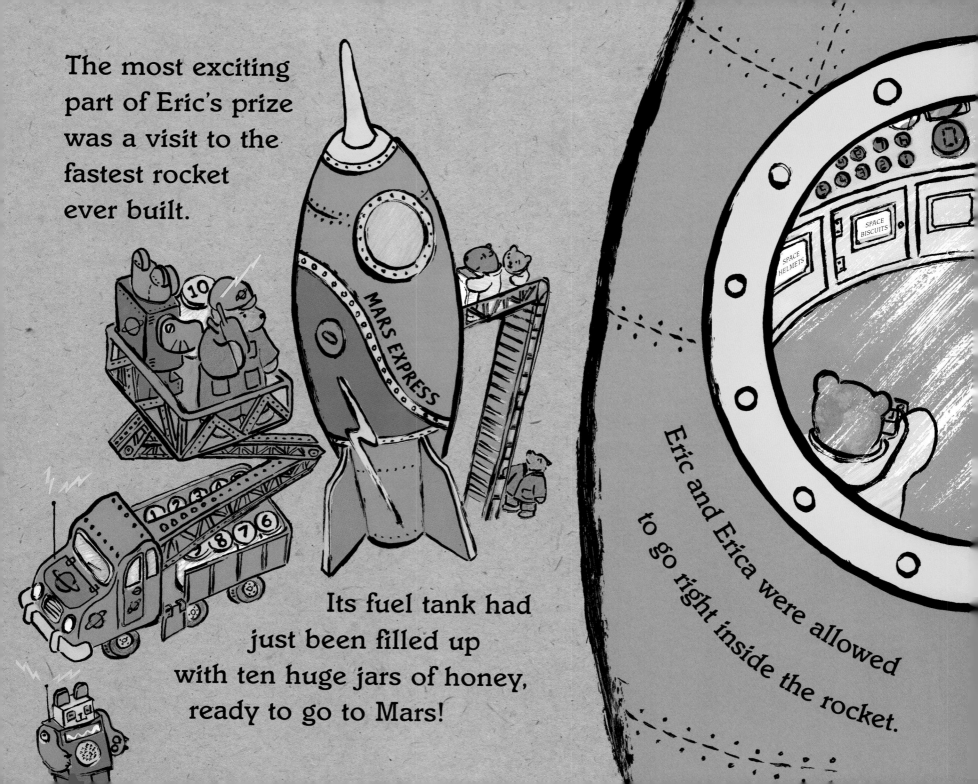

The most exciting part of Eric's prize was a visit to the fastest rocket ever built.

MARS EXPRESS

Its fuel tank had just been filled up with ten huge jars of honey, ready to go to Mars!

Eric and Erica were allowed to go right inside the rocket.

SPACE HELMETS

SPACE BISCUITS

Erica took lots of photos and Eric glowed very red.

Eric couldn't resist pressing some of the bright-red flashing numbers . . .

. . . just like a real astronaut counting down to . . .

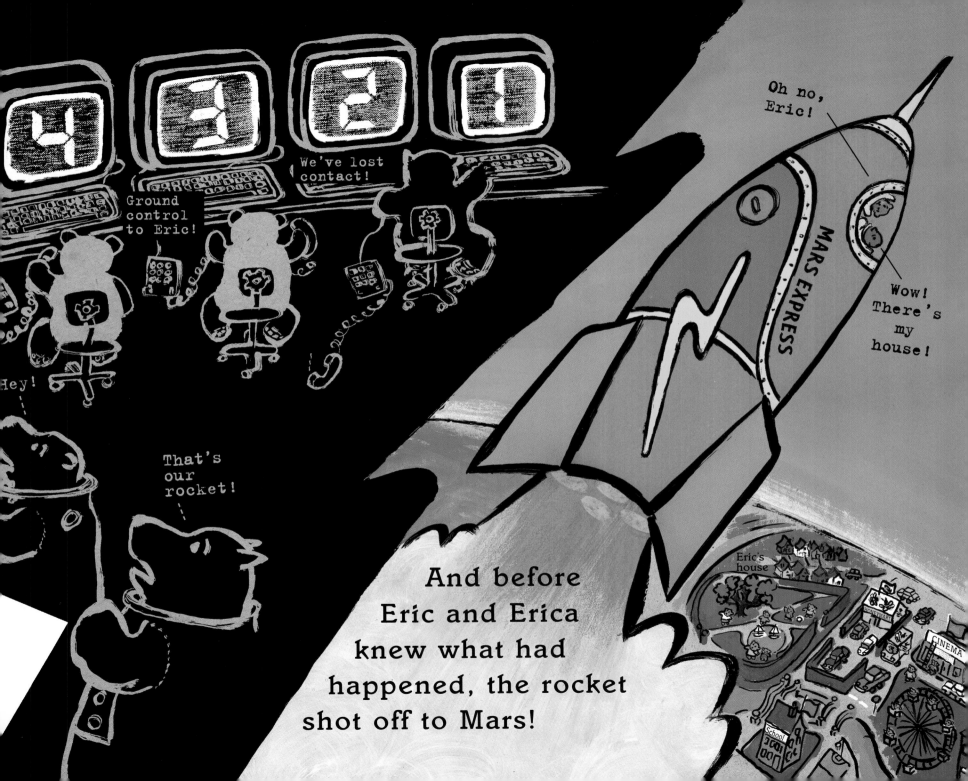

Eric and Erica
soon got the hang
of floating around
the cabin.

IN EMERGENCY CUT HOLE

WATER

FUE

Much better
than boring
space biscuits!

Asteroid Belt

Mars

Earth

SpaceBear
Universal Space
Map no.19

HONEY
NUMBER
PUFFS™

SPACE-O-METER

SPACE
BISCUITS

Before long
they were hungry.
Luckily, Erica found
ten huge jars of honey
in a cupboard.

Erica ate two
whole jars . . .

. . . and Eric
ate three.

(Well, it's a long
way to Mars.)

As soon as they landed on Mars,
Eric and Erica climbed out of
the rocket. They were the first
bears ever to set foot on
the red planet.

EXIT

LADDER

HAVE YOU
REMEMBERED
YOUR HELMET?

AIR

It's not as red
as I expected.

Erica took lots more photos.
Eric collected lots of rocks.

But it was very cold and Earth
looked a long way away.
Suddenly they felt lonely.
It was time to go home.

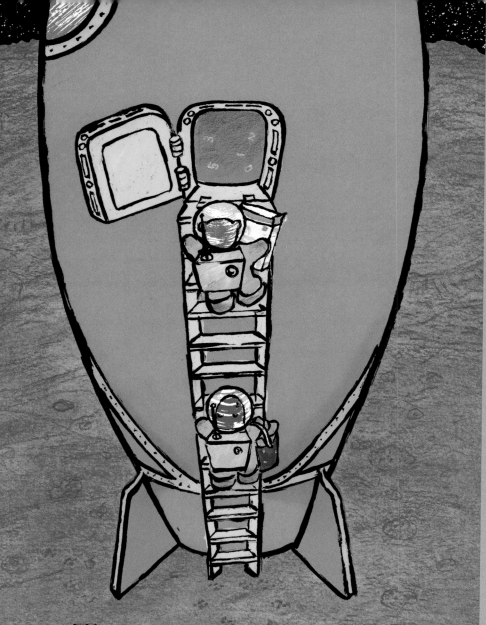

They climbed back
into the rocket. It was
much warmer inside.

"Ten seconds to lift off!"
said Eric. He counted down
just as before, pressing
each button in turn.

Nothing happened.
Eric couldn't understand
what was wrong.
He was sure he hadn't
made a mistake with
his counting.
Suddenly Erica
grabbed his paw.

"Look!" she gasped.
"The fuel tank! It's empty!
We're stuck on Mars!"

FUEL

EMPTY

FULL

UCKETS
SPADES

Eric thought
very hard.

The rocket had
used ten jars of
honey to fly to
Mars so . . .

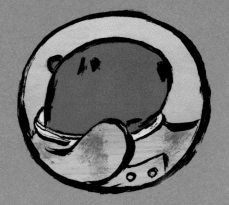

. . . it must need
another ten
to fly home.

"The honey . . ." he said, as he ran to
look in the cupboard.

There were only five jars left.
"Well, it's no use getting
halfway home," said Erica.
She licked her paw thoughtfully.

Then suddenly Erica started
jumping round the cabin.
"Eric!" she shouted.
"The dust on
my paws!
It's sweet!

# THERE'S
# HONEY
# ON
# MARS!"

Eric looked at the rocks he'd collected. They were melting. He gave one of them a careful lick. It was honey!

Luckily there was a saw for use in an emergency.

IN EMERGENCY CUT HOLE

SPACE MAPS

Once the tank's full, let's fill up all ten jars again. Then we can eat six on the way home...

Eric and Erica climbed back outside. They sawed a hole through the frozen rock. There was warm, gooey honey underneath!

... and we'll have four jars for our getting home party!

They filled up the five empty jars with honey. Now they had ten full jars, enough to fill the tank right up. Everything was very sticky and Eric glowed very red!

At last, they climbed back into the rocket. Eric took a deep breath and counted down once again ...

Phew! With a huge roar the rocket shot back towards Earth.

Eric and Erica floated happily around the cabin. "Well, I'm glad we didn't end up stuck on Mars," said Erica.

"I know," said Eric, licking a sticky Martian rock, "but imagine living on a planet made of honey!"

Erica smiled.
"Perhaps someone does," she said.

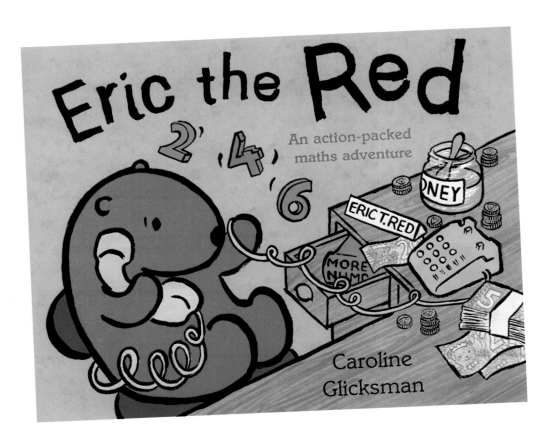